A BY DAWESY Book!

Johnson

A Day at the Museum

Written and created by

OLIVER DAWES

Illustrated by Snej Mommsen

ISBN 978-1-5272-1382-1

First published in the UK 2017

www.bydawesy.com

Printed and bound in the UK

HELLO? HELLO? HELLO?!
ARE YOU THERE? FOR I CAN'T SEE,
MY HEARING AND EYESIGHT AREN'T WHAT THEY USED TO BE.

LET ME INTRODUCE MYSELF, JOHNSON'S THE NAME,
DAYS OUT AND ADVENTURES ARE MY GAME!

MY BUTLER MONTY WILL LEAD THE WAY,
ALTHOUGH BETWEEN ME AND YOU I'VE SOMETHING TO SAY...

HE IS QUITE BORING AND ALWAYS BY MY SIDE,
SO I TEND TO WANDER OFF AND SOMETIMES HIDE!

COME ON LET'S GO! IT'S GETTING LATE,
I'M SO EXCITED I JUST CAN'T WAIT!

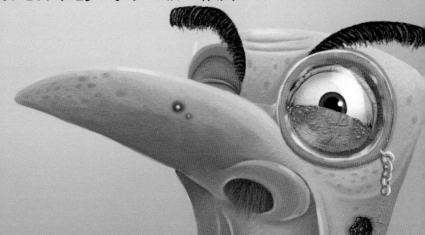

A DAY AT THE MUSEUM

SUCH WONDERFUL THINGS,
FROM PAINTINGS TO SCULPTURES
AND OLD GOLDEN RINGS.

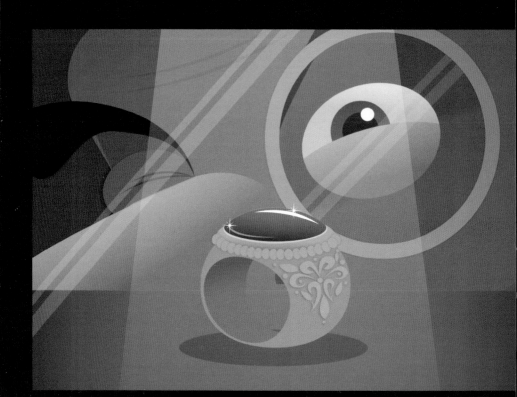

I'M **UPSTAIRS** I'M DOWNSTAIRS
I JUST **WANT** IT ALL,
LOOK AT THIS **PAINTING**;
I'M GLAD I'M SO **TALL!**

MONTY YOU FOOL, FOR I AM TALL,
I'LL DO WHAT I LIKE,

YOU'RE OLD AND SMALL.

NOW STAND BACK WILL YOU,

MY DEAR FRIEND,
YOUR NAGGING IS DRIVING ME ROUND THE BEND!

OH HELLO SIR, I'M SORRY TO SAY,
BUT YOU'RE FAR TOO CLOSE NOW STEP AWAY,

THIS PAINTING IS PRECIOUS AND VERY OLD,
SO EXPENSIVE IN FACT IT CAN'T BE SOLD!

THE NAME IS JOHNSON!
DO YOU KNOW WHO I AM?
A WEALTHY AND ARROGANT STUBBORN MAN!

I'LL DO AS I PLEASE, NOW TELL ME STAFF,
WHO IS THIS BY? I FIND IT NAFF.

OH SIR BE KIND, THIS ART IS FINE,
ITS BEAUTY AND QUALITY
WE SEE DOES SHINE.

THE ARTIST IS PURE,
SUCH TALENT AND MORE,

SNEJ IS HER NAME,
WRITTEN WITHIN THE FRAME.

NO NO NO!
NOW LET ME SHOW,
I'LL TAKE YOU ON A TOUR, COME ON LETS GO!

I'LL DANCE AND WEAVE,
JUMP AND BREATHE,
BECOME THE SHAPES
OF THE ARTISTS I NEED.

"REMBRANDT"

"PABLO PICASSO"

"GRANT WOOD"

"SALVADOR DALI"

"RENÉ MAGRITTE"

"EDVARD MUNCH"

"JOHANNES VERMEER"

"MICHELANGELO"

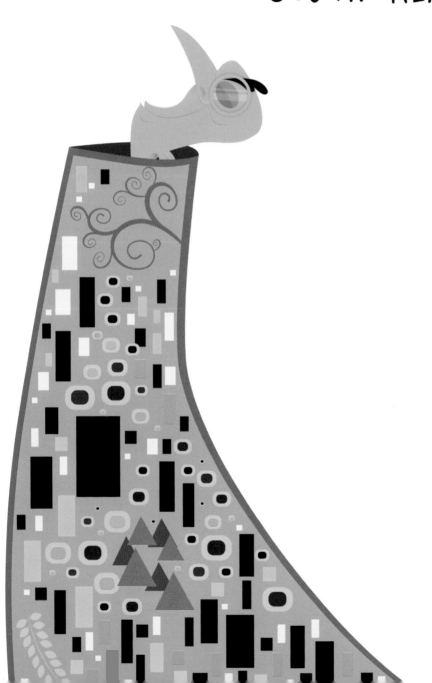

"GUSTAV KLIMT"

MY GOODNESS sir, WHAT A SHOW,
so MUCH we've LEARNT
AND NOW we KNOW.

THESE FAMOUS ARTISTS YOU
BECAME,

AND NOW WE KNOW THEM
NAME BY NAME!

NOT SO FAST, YOU'RE FORGETTING ONE,
AN ARTIST WHO PAINTS JUST FOR FUN,

HIS WORK IS AMAZING I'M SURE YOU'LL AGREE,
NOW YOU'RE BEGGING AND EXCITED TO SEE!

WHO COULD IT BE, OH LET US PLEASE!
WHEN WAITING I FIDGET AND JUMP LIKE A FLEA,
ANTS IN MY PANTS OR MAYBE A BEE,
WE CAN KEEP IT A SECRET,
JUST FOR US THREE!

JOHNSON'S THE NAME AND PAINTINGS MY GAME!
AS YOU CAN SEE FROM MY CREATIVITY.

COULD THIS BE, THE BEST PICTURE EVER?
DONE BY ME AS I'M SO CLEVER!
LOOK AT MY BEAUTY LOOK AT MY BOW,
TODAY HAS BEEN FUN, IT'S NOW TIME TO GO!